D0536173

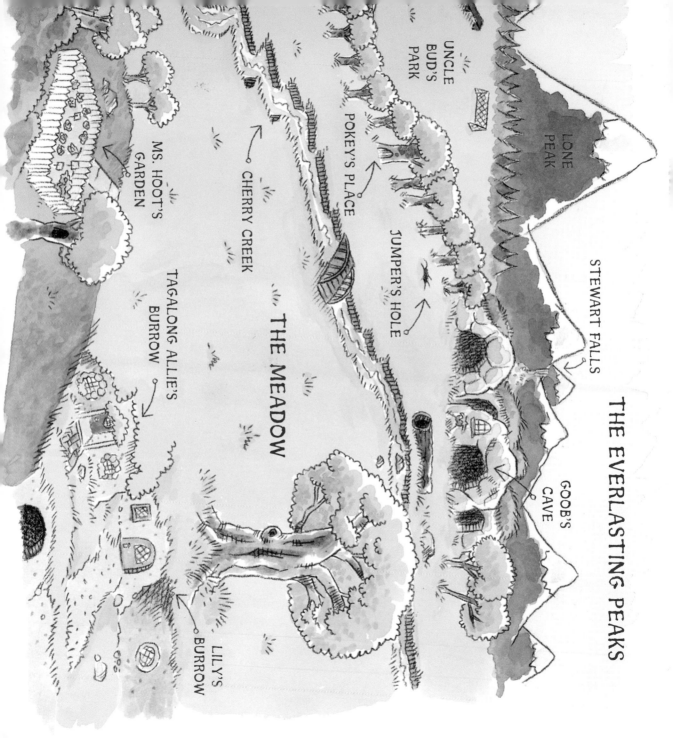

Just the Way I Am

To my daughter Victoria (a.k.a. Elle).

I love you just the way you are, full of life and oozing with proactivity.

—Sean Covey

For my beautiful wife, Jann—I love you just the way you are.

—Stacy Curtis

SIMON & SCHUSTER BOOKS FOR YOUNG READERS

An imprint of Simon & Schuster Children's Publishing Division

1230 Avenue of the Americas, New York, New York 10020

Copyright © 2009 by Franklin Covey Co.

All rights reserved, including the right of reproduction in whole or in part in any form.

SIMON & SCHUSTER BOOKS FOR YOUNG READERS is a trademark of Simon & Schuster, Inc.

For information about special discounts for bulk purchases, please contact Simon & Schuster Special Sales at 1-866-506-1949 or business@simonandschuster.com.

The Simon & Schuster Speakers Bureau can bring authors to your live event. For more information or to book an event, contact the Simon & Schuster Speakers Bureau at 1-866-248-3049 or visit our website at www.simonspeakers.com.

Also available in a Simon & Schuster Books for Young Readers hardcover edition

Book design by Laurent Linn

The text for this book was set in Montara Gothic.

The illustrations for this book were rendered in pencil and watercolor.

Manufactured in China | 0218 SCP

First Simon & Schuster Books for Young Readers paperback edition April 2018

2 4 6 8 10 9 7 5 3 1

The Library of Congress has cataloged the hardcover edition as follows:

Just the way I am / Sean Covey ; illustrated by Stacy Curtis.—1st ed.

p. cm. — (The seven habits of happy kids ; #1)

Summary: When Biff the beaver makes fun of Pokey's quills, his friends help the porcupine feel a lot better about himself.

ISBN 978-1-4169-9423-7 (hc alk. paper) | ISBN 978-1-5344-1577-5 (pbk) | ISBN 978-1-4424-9524-1 (eBook)

[1. Teasing—Fiction. 2. Schools—Fiction. 3. Self-esteem—Fiction.

4. Porcupines—Fiction. 5. Animals—Fiction.] I. Curtis, Stacy, ill. II. Title.

PZ7.C8343Ju 2009 | [E]—dc22 | 2009020744

Just the Way I Am

SEAN COVEY

Illustrated by **Stacy Curtis**

SIMON & SCHUSTER BOOKS FOR YOUNG READERS

New York   London   Toronto   Sydney   New Delhi

Pokey Porcupine was sad.

Every time he walked by Biff Beaver,

Biff made fun of him.

"Hey, Pokey. Your quills look like a pile

of toothpicks."

Pokey would go home and look in the mirror.

"Biff is right," thought Pokey. "My quills are ugly.

So ugly, I'm not going to school anymore."

His friends tried to help.

"I like your quills," said Goob Bear. "They're spiky."

"He's being outlandish," said Sophie Squirrel.

"Out-what?" said Sammy Squirrel.

"It means silly," said Sophie. "There's nothing wrong with your quills."

"I fink he's wude," said Tagalong Allie the mouse.

"You're a porcupine—you're supposed to have quills," said Jumper Rabbit.

"Just like I'm a rabbit—I'm supposed to be bouncy."

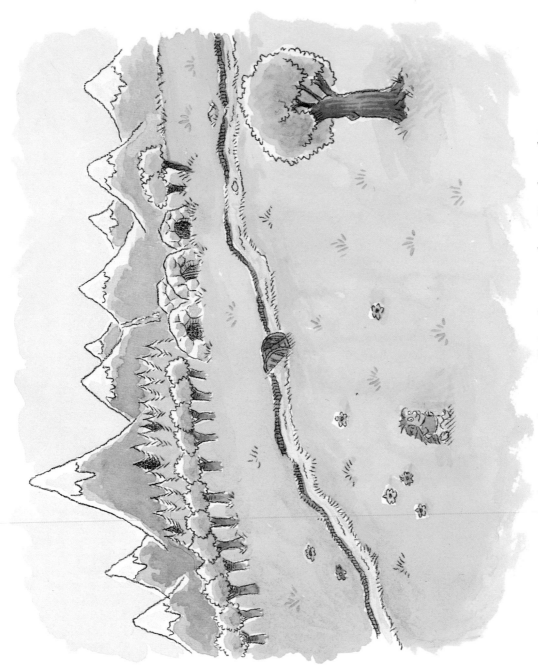

Pokey went for a walk in the meadow. He thought
about what his friends had said.

He stopped and looked at his reflection in Cherry Creek.

He wiggled his quills up. He wiggled his quills down.

They made a nice tinkly sound in the wind.

They sparkled in the sun.

Pokey decided that his quills weren't so bad. "I like myself," he thought, "just the way I am."

The next day, Pokey went back to school.

"How come your quills poke out so far?" said Biff.

Pokey smiled and walked away. He was not going

to let Biff ruin his day.

The next morning, Pokey decided he liked his quills so much,

he would show them off at school.

All of his friends gathered around him.

"I wish I had quills," said Biff.

PARENTS' CORNER

HABIT 1 —Be Proactive: *You're in Charge*

I REMEMBER WHEN MY LITTLE DAUGHTER DIDN'T WANT TO GO TO SCHOOL BECAUSE some girl had made fun of her freckles, or the time my son became self-conscious about his ears after a friend called him Dumbo. Ouch! The fact is, our kids are going to hear negative comments about themselves from time to time. We can't stop it from happening, but we can prepare them for it by teaching them that they do have a choice. They can let rude comments ruin their day or they can ignore them and replace them with positive self-talk. This doesn't mean that negative comments won't hurt. They always do. But we don't have to believe them or let them fester. Learning to be the master of our moods and to carry our own weather is one of the great challenges of life, even for us adults. But that is exactly what it means to be in charge of your own life, or to be proactive, which is the first habit of happy kids. We can't control what others say or do to us. But we can control what we do about it. And that is what counts. As Eleanor Roosevelt put it, "No one can make you feel inferior without your consent."

In this story, point out how all of us will have a bully like Biff or sometimes even a friend say something hurtful. And we can choose to let it bring us down or choose to shake it off, like water off a duck's back. In the end, Pokey made a good choice—he listened to his friends and his heart instead of listening to Biff.

Up for Discussion

1. Why was Pokey sad?

2. What did Pokey's friends do to try to make him feel better?

3. What helped Pokey like his quills again?

4. What did Pokey do when Biff Beaver made fun of his quills at school the next day?

5. Did Biff like Pokey's quills at the end of the story? What made Biff change his mind?

6. Has anyone ever said something to you that hurt your feelings? What did you do about it? Who is in charge of being happy or sad?

Baby Steps

1. The next time someone makes fun of you, smile and walk away, just like Pokey did.

2. Name three things you like about yourself.

3. Tell your mom or dad one thing you want to get better at, like drawing pictures or brushing your teeth.

4. If you hurt someone's feelings, like a friend or a brother or sister, make sure you tell them you're sorry.

THE SAND DUNES

THE EVERLASTING PEAKS

GOAT ISLAND

THE MISTY FOREST

BEAVER'S DAM

FAR NORTH WOODS

CHERRY CREEK

LOLLIGAG HILLS